To:

From:

ELMO GIVES THANKS

Words by Erin Guendelsberger
Pictures by Ernie Kwiat

SESAME STREET
sourcebooks wonderland

There's so much to be thankful for! Where do you start?

Everyday gratitude comes from the heart.

We're grateful for our bodies that work hard each day–
that help us to move, to grow, and to play.

We give thanks for good food that fills up our tummy
and cooking together to make meals that are yummy.

For sun in the summer and leaves in the fall,

winter snow, and spring flowers, we're glad for them all!

For time spent exploring the world all around–
we're thankful for all the adventures we've found.

We're grateful for giggles and silly things, too.
Smiling brings joy to me and to you!

We're thankful for kindness, for helping and caring—
for those who show love by their giving and sharing.

We love to create, to imagine and play.

We're thankful we think of new ideas each day!

We're grateful for learning, for teachers and schools–
our knowledge and wisdom are powerful tools!

DOGS!

There's so much we share, and we're each special, it's true.

Our differences make the whole world special, too!

Sometimes we make mistakes, some big and some small.
We're proud of ourselves and celebrate it all!

We're grateful for time spent with family and friends.

We cherish these moments from beginning to end.

We're thankful for love that fills up our hearts,
that we give and receive even when we're apart.

For a space that feels safe and a spot of our own,
we're thankful for that special place we call home.

We treasure all of these things and so many more.
All around us there's so much to be thankful for!

Words by Erin Guendelsberger
Illustrations by Ernie Kwiat

The full color art was completed using scanned traditional
pencil sketches rendered in Illustrator using a tablet.

Published by Sourcebooks Wonderland, an imprint of Sourcebooks Kids
P.O. Box 4410, Naperville, Illinois 60567-4410
(630) 961-3900
sourcebookskids.com

Cataloging-in-Publication Data is on file with the Library of Congress.

Source of Production: Wing King Tong Paper Products Co. Ltd., Shenzhen, Guangdong Province, China
Date of Production: March 2025
Run Number: 5049560

Printed and bound in China.
WKT 10 9 8 7 6 5 4 3 2